Animal Tales includes:

Hullabaloo!

Cub's First Summer

It's Following Me!

Little Grey Donkey

Look at me! Look at me!

PANdaMoNium

Hullabaloo!

Written by Gordon Volke
Illustrated by Alexia Orkrania

There's a donkey called Drew
Making a **hullabaloo** at the zoo.

There's a cockatoo who squawks out 'Boo!'
And a donkey called Drew
Making a *hullabaloo* at the zoo.

The chimp twins, Daisy and Maisie, enjoy their tea-for-two,
With the cockatoo who squawks out 'Boo!'
And a donkey called Drew

Making a *hullabaloo* at the zoo.

There are hopping bunnies with lots of grass to chew,
While the chimp twins, Daisy and Maisie, enjoy their tea-for-tw
With the cockatoo who squawks out 'Boo!'
And a donkey called Drew

Making a *hullabaloo* at the zoo.

There's a calf called Cassie who keeps on saying 'Moo!'
And hopping bunnies with lots of grass to chew,
While the chimp twins, Daisy and Maisie, enjoy their tea-for-two,
With the cockatoo who squawks out 'Boo!'
And a donkey called Drew

Making a *hullabaloo* at the zoo.

There are downy ducklings marching through!
Past a calf called Cassie who keeps on saying 'Moo!'
And hopping bunnies with lots of grass to chew,
While the chimp twins, Daisy and Maisie, enjoy their tea-for-two,
With the cockatoo who squawks out 'Boo!'
And a donkey called Drew

Making a *hullabaloo* at the zoo.

There's a roo called Sue with her joey, Blue,
who bounce around (that's all they do!)
And downy ducklings marching through!
Past a calf called Cassie who keeps on saying 'Moo!'
And hopping bunnies with lots of grass to chew,

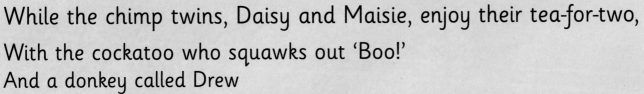

While the chimp twins, Daisy and Maisie, enjoy their tea-for-two,
With the cockatoo who squawks out 'Boo!'
And a donkey called Drew
Making a *hullabaloo* at the zoo.

There are baby owls who sit and say 'Twit-to-woo!'
Beside a roo called Sue with her joey, Blue,
who bounce around (that's all they do!)
And downy ducklings marching through!
Past a calf called Cassie who keeps on saying 'Moo!'
And hopping bunnies with lots of grass to chew,
While the chimp twins, Daisy and Maisie, enjoy their tea-for-two,
With the cockatoo who squawks out 'Boo!'
And a donkey called Drew

Making a *hullabaloo* at the zoo.

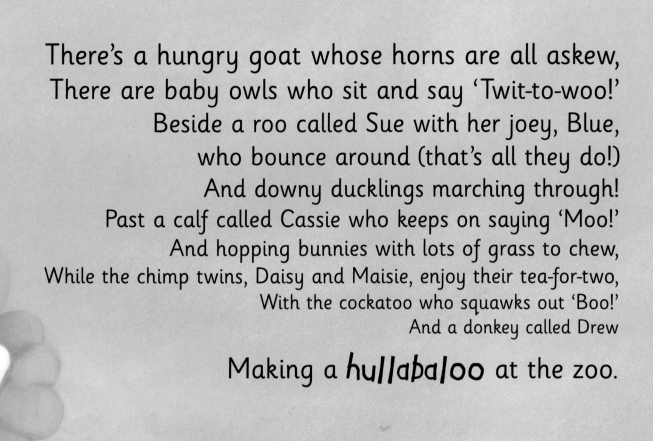

There's a hungry goat whose horns are all askew,
There are baby owls who sit and say 'Twit-to-woo!'
Beside a roo called Sue with her joey, Blue,
who bounce around (that's all they do!)
And downy ducklings marching through!
Past a calf called Cassie who keeps on saying 'Moo!'
And hopping bunnies with lots of grass to chew,
While the chimp twins, Daisy and Maisie, enjoy their tea-for-two,
With the cockatoo who squawks out 'Boo!'
And a donkey called Drew

Making a *hullabaloo* at the zoo.

Don't forget Dapple the horse – we must include him too!
There's a hungry goat whose horns are all askew,
There are baby owls who sit and say 'Twit-to-woo!'
Beside a roo called Sue with her joey, Blue,
who bounce around (that's all they do!)
And downy ducklings marching through!
Past a calf called Cassie who keeps on saying 'Moo!'
And hopping bunnies with lots of grass to chew,
While the chimp twins, Daisy and Maisie, enjoy their tea-for-two,
With the cockatoo who squawks out 'Boo!'
And a donkey called Drew

Making a *hullabaloo* at the zoo.

There's someone missing from the *hullabaloo* at the zoo!

Who?

You!

Cub's First Summer

by Rebecca Elliott

'For my little cubs – Clemmie and Toby. x'

It was the first day of summer and Cub had just woken up.
'Good morning,' said Mum. 'Let's go and explore the forest.
Come on …'

'Why is it so hot?'
asked Cub.

'So that we can splash in the cool water!' giggled Mum.

And the sun shone down.

'Why are the crickets
so loud?' asked Cub.

'Because they want us to jump
high like them!' exclaimed Mum.

And the sun grew hazy.

'Why are the days so long?'
asked Cub.

'So that we have more time for fun!' laughed Mum.

And the sunlight began to fade.

'Why are there so many flowers?' asked Cub.
'So that we can enjoy their beautiful smell!' sniffed Mum.

And clouds began
to gather in the sky.

'Why are the birds singing
so loudly?' asked Cub.

'So that we can dance to their music!' sang Mum.

And the clouds got darker.

'Why are the bees so busy?' asked Cub.
'Because they want to make us lots of
yummy honey!' said Mum.

And the air
grew heavy.

'Why are the vegetables so big?' asked Cub.

'So that we can feast on them!' spluttered Mum,
with her mouth full of carrot.
And the first flash of lightning lit up the sky.

'What's that noise?' asked Cub, as the first rumble
of thunder grumbled all around him.

'Oh no!' gasped Mum.
'Quick! Follow me before the thunderstorm gets worse!'

And back they went through the vegetable patch, past the trees, back and forth through the meadow, and over the river until, at last, they found their way home!

'Why is the thunderstorm
so scary?' asked Cub.

'So that we can
snuggle up tight,'
whispered Mum,
with a smile.

'Why am I so tired?' yawned Cub.
'Because it is sleepy time,'
murmured Mum.
'Night night, little cub.'

It's Following Me!

by Sheri Radford

'To Katya and all the other feisty felines who have
left their paw prints on my heart.'
Sheri Radford

It's behind me in the kitchen,
It's behind me in the hall,
It's behind me when I'm leaping,
It's behind me when I fall.

It follows me in the darkness,
It follows me in the sun,
It follows me when I'm feeling sad,
Or when I'm having fun.

It's behind me when I'm sleeping,
It's behind me when I wake,
It's behind me in the garden,
It's behind me by the lake.

It follows me when I'm walking,
Or running down the hall,
It follows me when I'm pouncing,
Or pressed up against the wall.

I wonder why it follows me?
I wonder why it tries?
I need a good detective,
Or several clever spies.

I've tried to ignore it,
I've tried not to stare,
I've tried to pretend,
That I just don't care.

But it's behind me when I'm eating,
It's behind me when I nap,
It's behind me when I'm meowing,
Or when I'm curled up on a lap.

I've tried at times to run away,
I've even tried to flee,
But it seems that everywhere I go,
It always follows me!

It's behind me in the basement,
It's behind me on the stairs,
It's behind me on the sofa,
It's behind me on the chairs.

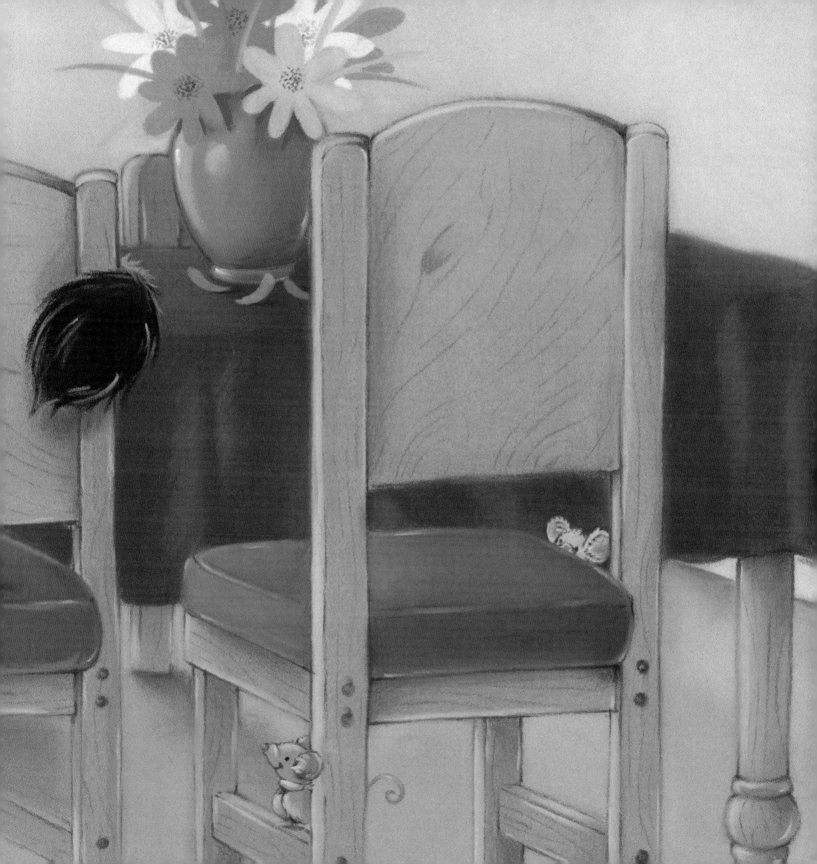

It's really rather funny looking,
Sticking straight up in the air.
It doesn't matter where I go,
It always is right there.

If I remain alert,
And stay on my guard,
Then I'm sure to catch it,
And I'll bite it hard.

Ouch!

Little Grey Donkey

Written by Nicole Snitselaar
Illustrated by Coralie Saudo

In the middle of the big, blue sea,
there is a little island.
And on that little island,
lived Little Grey Donkey.

Every day, a little girl called Sérafina came to visit Little Grey Donkey. She always brought some nice crunchy carrots and they enjoyed playing together in the shade of the green cypress trees.

But one day, Sérafina did not
come and visit Little Grey Donkey!
No crunchy carrots, no games,
no loving words whispered in his ear.
Little Grey Donkey was very upset.

Little Grey Donkey waited
and waited for Sérafina to arrive.
Many bright mornings and dark nights followed.
'Where is Sérafina? Why doesn't she come?'
wondered Little Grey Donkey.
Little Grey Donkey was worried about Sérafina,
and so he decided to go and look for her.

The path Little Grey Donkey followed
was very narrow and terribly steep!
'I can't go on! I'm too scared,' cried Little Grey Donkey.
Then he remembered Sérafina, swallowed his fears,
and bravely started down the track.

Further along, Little Grey Donkey discovered a skateboard at the edge of a very steep cliff. 'This cliff is too steep. I'm going to fall and hurt myself!' cried Little Grey Donkey. Then he remembered Sérafina, swallowed his fears, sat on the skateboard and raced down the slope.

Once Little Grey Donkey reached the bottom of the cliff, he discovered that the only way to go further was to climb into a small boat. 'Me? In a boat? I'm much too scared to do that!' cried Little Grey Donkey. Then he remembered Sérafina, swallowed his fears and got into the boat.

Using all of his strength, Little Grey Donkey rowed across
the sea and discovered a small village perched on
the top of the cliffs.
'Must I use this rusty brown lift? Never!
I might fall down or get stuck,' cried Little Grey Donkey.
Then he remembered Sérafina, swallowed his fears,
climbed on the lift and was hoisted to the top.

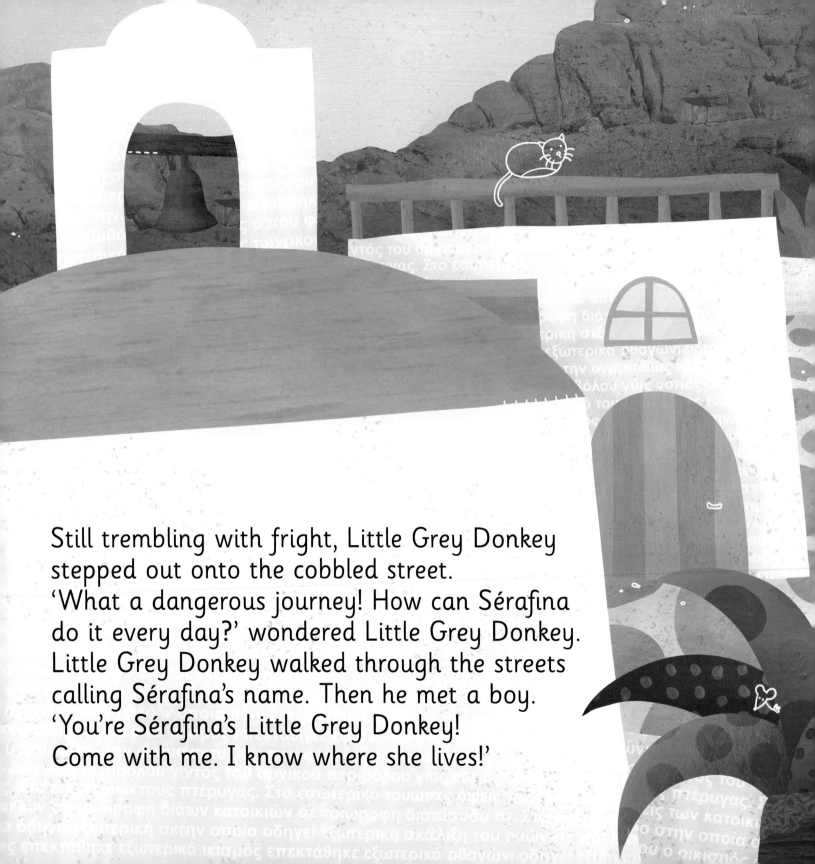

Still trembling with fright, Little Grey Donkey
stepped out onto the cobbled street.
'What a dangerous journey! How can Sérafina
do it every day?' wondered Little Grey Donkey.
Little Grey Donkey walked through the streets
calling Sérafina's name. Then he met a boy.
'You're Sérafina's Little Grey Donkey!
Come with me. I know where she lives!'

Καλημέρα

81

Σεραφι

Sérafina had been ill and was resting on the rooftop terrace of her house. 'Little Grey Donkey! You came all this way to visit me,' she cried with surprise.

'How did you manage it?' asked Sérafina.
Sérafina knew all about the narrow
mountain track, the steep cliff, the boat,
and the rusty lift.
Little Grey Donkey smiled up at Sérafina.
'I thought of you, swallowed my fears,
and was filled with ...

Φιλία

… love.'

Look at me!
Look at me!

Written by Rose Williamson
Illustrated by Doreen Marts

Cammy Chameleon lived in a tree and was very good at hiding. Cammy turned brown on a brown branch and green on a green leaf.

It made it very easy to sneak up on yummy bugs!

But Cammy didn't want to hide. She thought she was a very beautiful chameleon indeed and she wanted all of the other animals to look at her.

She called out to the tree frogs,
'Look at me! Look at me!'

But the tree frogs could
not see a green chameleon
on a green leaf.

She called out to the lemurs,
'Look at me! Look at me!'

But the lemurs could not see a brown
chameleon on a brown branch.

Cammy was very upset that no one could see her.
She began to wonder what it would be like if
she didn't always blend in ...

Cammy climbed down from her tree and concentrated very, very hard ...

And turned red!

'Look at me! Look at me!'
she called to the tree frogs.
'What a beautiful chameleon!' they said.

Cammy practised changing colour all day.
She was pink on a grey stone ...

She was black on yellow sand ...

She was purple on
an orange flower …

… and orange on
a purple flower.

'Look at me! Look at me!'
she called to the lemurs.
'What a beautiful
chameleon!' they said.

Cammy thought she was
the most beautiful chameleon
in the whole world.

Soon, she began to feel hungry
and went home to her tree.

Cammy climbed onto her brown branch and waited for a yummy bug. She waited and waited.

She watched the other chameleons catching bugs on their sticky tongues and her stomach rumbled. She was very hungry!

Then, Cammy saw a group of bugs nearby!
But, before she could stick out her long
tongue, they saw her beautiful
colours and flew away!

'What a beautiful chameleon!'
the laughing bugs called to her.

Suddenly, Cammy felt very silly.
A colourful chameleon couldn't hide
like a plain brown chameleon!

Cammy knew that to catch bugs,
she would need to blend in so she
concentrated very, very hard ...

and changed colour so that she
blended in with her surroundings!

Cammy had learnt that it is not good to show off and was happy being a regular chameleon again.

But sometimes, just every once in a while,
Cammy concentrates very, very hard ...

PANdAMONium

Written by Dan Crisp   Illustrated by Mark Chambers

For Mum, Dad and Caleb Crisp - Dan
For Lucinda, who smells great! - M.C

As the zookeeper snored,
The great lion roared,

And the octopus borrowed the keys.

With tentacles nimble,
he found it quite simple, to open the locks with some ease.

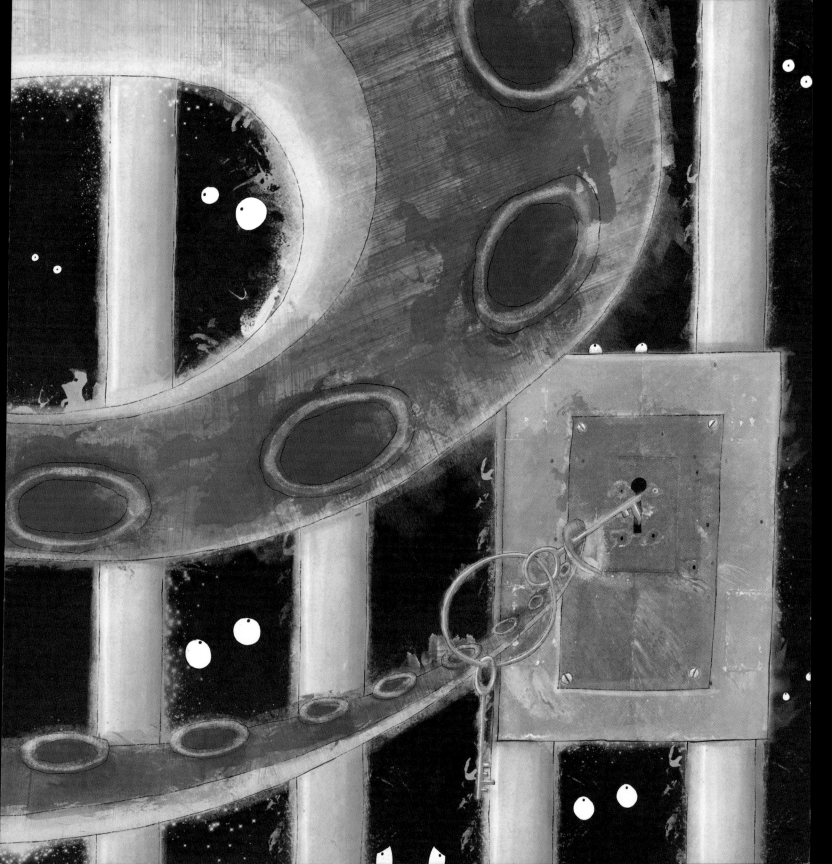

When all the animals were freed,
The pandas agreed,

That the party
should really begin.

The flamingos' excitement,

PARTY!

At the pandas'
announcement,

Caused the hyenas to grin.

A change in the mood!
PANDAmonium ensued!

Rousing even
the dodo from sleep.

A party all round!
And despite all
the sound,

From the zookeeper;
still not a peep.

But just then the skunk,
(who was dressed as a punk)

Nasty pong

↓

Did such an unsavoury thing.

'Now, who's made that stink?'
Said the polecat to the mink,
As their eyes were beginning to sting.

'Back to your cages!
That pong will stay for ages!'

Squealed the elephant, knotting his trunk.

On detecting the smell,
The turtle put his head in his shell,

And the monkey jumped back in his bunk.

But then the zookeeper's nose,
And the tips of his toes,

Suddenly started to twitch.

He pricked up his ears,
And his eyes filled with tears,
At the odour that was so very rich.

Twitchy
nose

The Daily Zoo
SKUNK STILL
SMELLS!

He woke from his dreams,
Said, 'I'm giving up beans!'

And returned to
reading his paper.